W9-AYY-824

BIRD
SPRINGS

Carolyn Marsden

VIKING

VIKING
Published by Penguin Group
Penguin Young Readers Group, 345 Hudson Street, New York, New York 10014, U.S.A.
Penguin Group (Canada), 90 Eglinton Avenue East, Suite 700, Toronto, Ontario,
Canada M4P 2Y3 (a division of Pearson Penguin Canada Inc.)
Penguin Books Ltd, 80 Strand, London WC2R 0RL, England
Penguin Ireland, 25 St Stephen's Green, Dublin 2, Ireland (a division of Penguin Books Ltd)
Penguin Group (Australia), 250 Camberwell Road, Camberwell, Victoria 3124,
Australia (a division of Pearson Australia Group Pty Ltd)
Penguin Books India Pvt Ltd, 11 Community Centre, Panchsheel Park,
New Delhi – 110 017, India
Penguin Group (NZ), 67 Apollo Drive, Mairangi Bay, Auckland 1311, New Zealand
(a division of Pearson New Zealand Ltd)
Penguin Books (South Africa) (Pty) Ltd, 24 Sturdee Avenue, Rosebank,
Johannesburg 2196, South Africa

Penguin Books Ltd, Registered Offices: 80 Strand, London WC2R 0RL, England

First published in 2007 by Viking, a division of Penguin Young Readers Group

1 3 5 7 9 10 8 6 4 2

LIBRARY OF CONGRESS CATALOGING-IN-PUBLICATION DATA
Marsden, Carolyn.
Bird Springs / by Carolyn Marsden.
p. cm.
Summary: When drought and his father's absence force them to leave the Navajo
reservation at Bird Springs, ten-year-old Gregory, his mother, and sister move to a motel
in Tuscon, Arizona, where one of Gregory's teachers helps him confront his painful past.
ISBN-13: 978-0-670-06193-8 (hardcover)
[1. Moving, Household—Fiction. 2. Shelters for the homeless—Fiction.
3. Schools—Fiction. 4. Family problems—Fiction. 5. Navajo Indians—Fiction.
6. Indians of North America—Arizona—Fiction. 7. Arizona—Fiction.] I. Title.
PZ7.M35135Bir 2007
[Fic]—dc22
2006029071

Printed in U.S.A.
Set in New Aster
Book design by Sam Kim

For Timothy and Wyatt,
and for the children of Mission View School

Gregory kicked a pebble between the bars of the grate made of crisscrossing iron. The grate covered a hole in the school lawn. The pebble dropped, tumbling down and down. Gregory listened until it made its final plunk, then glanced at his sister, Jeanine, drinking a bottle of formula, holding it all by herself.

Mom stood with her hands on the handles of the stroller. "Good-bye, honey," she said. "I'll be thinking of you." She raised her hands as though to offer him a hug, then lifted her thick braid off her shoulder instead.

Gregory wanted a hug, wanted to relax against Mom for a moment, but other kids might see. "Bye," he said, and walked up the ramp. He pulled back the heavy door and didn't look back.

The teacher stood by her desk, tall and red-haired. When she saw him, she picked up a piece of paper. "You must be the new student," she said, holding the registration form lightly between her long pale fingers.

He nodded, pushing his long black hair out of his eyes.

Fifth-graders sat around the tables with lumps of gray modeling clay. But no one was working. They stared at Gregory. Here in Tucson, Arizona, in this unfamiliar classroom, he would have to get to know all new people.

"I'm Ms. Daniels," the teacher said, leading him to an empty spot.

The boy beside him had light hair shaved so short that Gregory could hardly tell the color. The boy pushed some of his clay to Gregory's spot.

At first, Gregory pretended he didn't see the clay. The kid was being too friendly, too fast.

Ms. Daniels leaned down, and Gregory could smell the coolness of her. Not perfume or soap but like the wind passing over the snow on Deer Creek Pass.

"We're exploring the clay, Gregory. You don't have to make anything yet. Just experiment for now."

Without looking at the blond boy, Gregory smooshed the clay, first with one hand, then the other. He knew the boy and the other kids were studying him, but he didn't look up. He wasn't sure he wanted to make real friends.

Mom had explained that they could only stay in the motel for thirty days. Two of those days were already gone. He'd left the reservation only three days ago, but it felt like three hundred years.

Beside him sat Joey. Joey was ten like him, Navajo like him. Like him, he'd grown until his pants rode above his ankles. Joey liked exactly the same things that Gregory liked. When the rains had stopped, Gregory had discovered Joey. Now Joey seemed so real that Gregory could sense his presence like a shimmer of air. He had to be careful not to talk out loud to Joey, because other kids couldn't see him.

"Why aren't you making anything?" the blond boy asked, leaning over onto Gregory's side. With squarish fingers he held out a rough-looking bowl. His chunky hand grazed Gregory's thin brown one.

"I'm just exploring. Like the miss said." Gregory squeezed so hard that the clay burst between his fingers.

"Suit yourself. My name's Matt."

Gregory pushed his hair out of his eyes and made himself look straight up into the boy's wide, tanned face.

"You can sit with me at lunch," Matt said.

Gregory nodded and Joey nodded, too. They couldn't do more. Gregory felt like a leaf floating in the wash at Bird Springs when the rains came. The current could bump him up against this rock or that, or sink him altogether.

This was the first time he'd ever left the reservation. The reservation lay up north and touched the bottom of the state of Utah. Here in the city, he'd never seen so many buildings, such tall buildings, so many cars, so many white people. The earth was gray and brown instead of red. Rather than going to a big school like this one, the kids of the reservation traveled across the mesa to meet together in one room.

Gregory kept passing the clay from one hand to the other. When Matt wasn't looking, he secretly broke off an imaginary piece and passed it to Joey.

He concentrated on feeling his feet against the carpeted floor, his legs against the chair, warming it as he sat, holding the damp weight of his clay. His sneakers had holes where his big toes rubbed. When he took a peek at Matt's shoes, he saw the sides of Matt's big toes poking through as well.

"I'll tell you a secret," said Matt.

Gregory leaned a fraction of an inch closer.

"This isn't just an art class. This is called art *therapy*. The teacher thinks she can heal up all our problems with clay and stuff. Only the screwed-up people come here."

Screwed-up people? Did that mean him? Gregory looked down at the front of his clean blue shirt, at his legs disappearing under the table. His jeans had a tear over each knee. How had the school decided he was screwed up? Was it because he was Navajo? Was it because he came from the reservation? Or was it . . . ? But he didn't want to think about that.

And this boy, Matt. Was *he* screwed up?

Gregory looked at Ms. Daniels, her clear glass earrings glinting in the light from the window. Had *she* made the decision?

"In a minute, the bell'll ring and we go to our regular teachers," Matt said.

Gregory gripped his clay with both hands. He didn't want to go anywhere else. Not yet.

Ms. Daniels walked to the front of the classroom. "Boys and girls, please pass your clay to the person on your right."

As the clay was being collected, Ms. Daniels came to Gregory's table. "Here's your school back-pack," she said. She laid the bright red backpack on the desk in front of him and unzipped it.

Matt helped him discover the treasures inside: two kinds of notebooks, fancy pencils, a glue stick, and even a small candy bar and a Fruit Roll-Up.

Gregory's hand brushed against Joey's, since Joey was eager to explore the treasures as well.

When the bell rang and he had to leave, Gregory put the backpack on his back, taking a little bit of Ms. Daniels's class with him. The pack was heavy and almost comforting.

2

Across the grass, in another classroom, Mr. Best passed out tubs of counting cubes. "We're going to work with our fractions in a new way, kiddos." He held up a green cube. "And no throwing these."

Matt was with a different teacher, so Gregory sat alone.

While Mr. Best was writing numbers on the board, Gregory secretly counted out thirty cubes. Then he took away two.

Twenty-eight days until he would have to move.

He didn't look up to meet anyone's eyes. With so few days, it wasn't worth it to make friends. Lots of the boys had shaved heads. None had long hair like he did. But like him, all the kids had clothes with stains and rips.

At St. John's Indian School, they didn't have counting cubes. Instead, Mr. Flores handed out sheets of number problems, then leaned over the kids one by one, putting red checks by wrong answers. When the heater wasn't working, Gregory had felt like writing a wrong answer on purpose so that Mr. Flores would stand behind him for a moment longer, protecting him against the cold.

During social studies, Mr. Best taught about ancient Egypt. He pointed to a map, at an irregular orange patch. "This is the country, boys and girls. We're not studying it as it is now but the way it was many, many years ago." Mr. Best wore a stiff bow tie at his throat.

Behind him, Gregory heard someone say, "Mr. Best looks like *he* came from ancient Egypt."

Mr. Best turned on his computer and showed pictures of sandy red landscapes that reminded Gregory of Bird Springs.

Joey strained to see the hieroglyphics.

As the images of Egypt slipped along, Gregory took peeks at the posters on the wall: a tall, lacy tower that leaned to the right; people dancing with golden cones on their heads; a huge sweep of green water he guessed was the ocean.

And outside this room, the city breathed, an expanse as foreign to him as ancient Egypt. It pulsed with even, mechanical energies—the traffic, the refrigerators, the hum of the school air-conditioning—different from the random coyote cries and birdcalls, the occasional drop of a pine-cone, the swish of the wind at Bird Springs.

Bird Springs was no more than a cluster of small houses. Even the trading post lay miles down the highway. Only Gregory's family and a handful of relatives lived there. Or had. Now Bird Springs was probably abandoned.

As Mr. Best showed pictures of the pyramids from different angles, Gregory closed his eyes to ancient Egypt. The world was mysterious enough already.

Noise rushed through the cafeteria like a flash flood.

"We wait here," Matt said, pointing to a spot in the line. "When you get close to the ladies, shout out what you want."

At St. John's Indian School, the kids brought their own lunches. Except on Wednesdays when the moms got together and made hamburgers for sale. "How do I know what I want?"

"It says it right there." Matt pointed to a white board. "Steak fingers or chicken bits."

Joey stood near Gregory and talked to him mind-to-mind: *Don't be afraid to eat. You'll need energy to do schoolwork in the afternoon.*

Joey was a baby thing, but he couldn't help it.

Matt led the way to a table. "Where do you come from anyhow?" he asked as they settled their trays.

"From the reservation."

"Hey, cool. Does that mean you're a real Indian?"

Gregory swung his leg over the bench and nodded.

"You Indian guys still eat bear meat?" Matt asked.

Gregory shook his head. "I've never had bear meat." He picked up a tater tot.

A boy a few seats down pointed with his breadstick. "Look at your hair, dude. It's so long."

Gregory recognized the boy from Mr. Best's class.

"Yeah, you need a haircut," said Matt.

"It looks like a bush." The boy ate half the breadstick in one bite.

"Or a wig," said Matt, laughing so hard that a chicken bit shot out of his mouth.

Gregory slumped down and tried to laugh with them. His cheeks got hot. He knew his long hair looked ugly. It had been months since Mom had cut it, setting him on the chair outside, winter or summer, clipping and clipping, as she might a sheep, while the black hair fell down the back of his shirt.

But why had Matt joined the boy in teasing him? Wasn't Matt his new friend?

The boy had just gotten a head shave like Matt. Joey noticed. *Baldie!* he shouted. But only Gregory could hear.

Gregory finished up his canned peaches.

Honeydew Head! Joey shouted at the boy.

Gregory kicked Joey under the table.

What Gregory couldn't tell anyone, especially Mom, was that he was growing his hair long like Dad's. Dad wore his in a long ponytail bound all the way along with strips of leather strung with turquoise and silver beads. If he looked enough like Dad, maybe Dad would find him.

"His last name is Begay. Get it? *Be gay!*" Matt chortled loudly.

"Be gay, be gay," chanted the boy, fluttering his hands.

Everyone at the table giggled.

Talking about his hair was one thing. Dad's name was another. Gregory got up and dumped his food st

ng

ers

gory
and.

back to the motel
came through the   noes,"
carrying a full can

took care of the   ld see
a mermaid tat
flexed his arm,   vard. "It
ook, sonny. Just
he first day. But   eing all
at the trading
g tattoos. Later,   an Indian
it wasn't a gang
gotten while he

After school, Gregory walked beside the freeway. When he motel gate, he spotted Mr. Hass of trash.

Mr. Hass, the house manager place. He had a silver flattop an tooed on his forearm. When he the mermaid seemed to swim. "I like she's in the ocean," he'd said Gregory had stepped back. On T post, he'd seen bad people wearin Mom told him not to be afraid, that tattoo, but one that Mr. Hass had was a sailor.

"How's it going, son?" Mr. Hass set down the trash can. His long sleeves covered the mermaid.

"Okay."

"Not getting into any trouble, I hope."

Gregory shook his head. "Nope. I have too much homework."

"Good. Study hard. It's the only way out." Mr. Hass picked up the trash and headed for the Dumpster. Then he turned back. "By the way, son. See those bushes?" He pointed to a tall hedge with sharp leaves and fluffy pink blossoms. "Those are oleanders. Very poisonous. Don't let your baby sister eat any."

"No, sir," Gregory said.

He fitted his key in the lock of the brown door. The door had a hole punched in it, just fist height. He swung the door open and walked into the motel room. There were two twin beds—one for him and one for Mom, each with a milky-blue bedspread— and a crib in the corner for Jeanine.

Propped on the round table was a note from Mom: I'M OUT HUNTING FOR A JOB, HONEY. OK TO LEAVE J IN DAY CARE.

He pulled the heavy curtains shut and lay down

on his narrow bed. After a moment, he moved toward the wall so there would be room for Joey.

The weather was still hot down here in the city. But in Bird Springs, the cottonwoods along the dry wash would be turning yellow, their leaves flashing back and forth in the sunshine. He could hear the squeak of the big gate where Dad's truck pulled in and out. He smelled the sage, spicy and sharp, as the sheep brushed through it coming back down to the pen.

Gregory rolled over and sat up. From his new backpack, he took the crayons—red, blue, and yellow—wrapped in cellophane. He handed the yellow to Joey since it was Joey's favorite color. Gregory took out one of the sheets of paper and began to draw Batman. He sketched in the details: the belt at the narrow waist, the boots, the mask. He cut the figure out. And then he added wings, attaching them with the glue stick.

He'd been drawing Batman ever since he was a little kid at St. John's Indian School. In the after-school program there, he'd watched the movie of Batman flying through the night sky. He'd imagined himself flying just like that, powerful and free. Now he didn't think so much about flying but drew the figures out of habit.

He drew a Batman of each color. He started to slip them into a shoe box he kept full of Batmen, but changed his mind and tucked them into his new backpack instead.

Dad had taught him how to draw. As a little boy, Gregory sat in his lap while Dad sketched the sheep grazing in the high pasture or the flat land and jagged buttes of the next valley. Sometimes he drew Gregory's face. Gregory had kept the drawings in a folder. Now he leaned down and pulled the folder out from under the bed. He opened to a portrait of himself. He remembered the day Dad drew it. Snow had been flurrying outside, the woodstove burning high. Dad had looked at him so carefully while he penciled in the eyes, the eyebrows. . . . Gregory placed his palm gently across the picture before slipping the folder back under the bed.

He and Dad used to ride Blackie together. Blackie was all black except for a triangle of white on his forehead. When Gregory was in the saddle up front, he'd felt Dad's breath on the back of his neck as they rode through the sage, over the red sand,

Dad's hand on his waist as they curved this way and that. *My only son,* Dad had said.

Once Dad had surprised him at St. John's, coming for him on Blackie. They'd ridden Blackie home across the mesa. Gregory had watched the yellow school bus in the distance, making its way along the highway, dropping off kids in the gray afternoon.

Maybe Dad would look for him here, would find him. With Dad, everything would be easier.

What was holding Dad up? Why hadn't he come?

Gregory went outside. As trucks whistled past on the freeway, he wandered up and down the paths in the patio of the motel. The flower gardens weren't kept nice. The soil had been covered over with gravel, and he guessed that no one wanted to take care of anything extra.

Joey skipped gravel pebbles along the sidewalk.

All the paths led to the swimming pool, which was just a chained-off cement hole with no water. It would have been fun to have a pool in this hot weather.

When Gregory was little, the monsoons had

come, and the pool up by Standing Rock had filled up. On steamy mornings, after the summer rain had passed, you could jump off the rock and make a big splash and land in the deep green water. Matt would like that.

Just as Gregory thought about Matt, he noticed that Joey frowned a little. Then he remembered how Matt had turned against him in the cafeteria. Maybe he wouldn't invite Matt to Standing Rock after all.

The only real thing the paths led to was a soda machine, red and humming under a roof built just for it.

At St. John's, whenever summer vacation drew near, kids penciled lines on their notebooks, tallying the days left until they'd be set free.

Gregory found a sharp little rock and, on the back of the machine, where no one would care, he scratched twenty-eight marks. He didn't group the lines by fives because he wanted to mark them out one by one.

Mr. Hass wouldn't like you doing that, Joey whispered.

Gregory swung around to look for Mr. Hass. No one in sight.

Gregory walked slowly back and forth on the path. He scanned the sky for clouds. Maybe rain would come. He loved the feel of the rain on his face, the sound it made hitting the tin roof of the house, the sweet smells of the juniper and sage when it rained. Mom had told him that if it rained here it would rain at Bird Springs.

If it rained enough at Bird Springs, Gregory figured, they could move back. Dad would find a way to join them.

But there was just blue and more blue in all directions.

He went back into the motel room—through the broken door—and sat down at the round table with his social studies textbook. When opened, it covered the whole Formica surface. He looked at the red sand, the pyramids, the Sphinx. One photo showed the Nile River, a wide band of blue in the desert. Dry as the place looked, it still had life flowing through it. He thought again of the pool at Standing Rock and how for two summers it'd been dry.

That evening after Mom had tucked Jeanine into her crib, Gregory sat down next to her on the bed. He put his hand on her arm so that she wouldn't get up. "I need to know about Dad," he said.

She turned to look at him, her face smooth in spite of her worries, her black hair glossy, then dropped her gaze to the bed. "What about Dad?" she asked.

"Where is he? When will we see him again? Will he come here?" He rushed the questions out in one breath.

Mom put a hand on each of her knees and straightened her arms. "You've asked me these things before, Gregory. I still don't know the answers. I haven't heard a word."

"But what about Auntie Mary? Can't you call her and ask?"

"Gregory"—Mom laughed quickly without smiling—"you've gotten too used to the city. Auntie Mary has no phone."

"Couldn't we go back and live with Johnny?"

Mom shook her head no. A strand of her hair fell loose. "Johnny and his family are having a hard time, too. Who knows if they're even still there. Until it rains, and rains for a good long time, no one can live easily at Bird Springs."

Gregory could feel the lumps of the bedspread against the backs of his legs. The lumps made patterns of lines and diamond shapes. "But how—" He stopped and swallowed a pocket of tears. "Why did Dad go off like that and leave us?"

Mom pulled him close to her. The bed sagged, and the two leaned heavily against each other. "The drought, hon. The drought was extra hard on the men. They didn't know how to take care of us." She put her arm around him. "You've been so brave, coming here, making a new start. How was school?"

Gregory shrugged. He didn't want to tell her about being put into Ms. Daniels's class for screwed-up kids.

He moved away from Mom, over to the round table. He opened his math book. At least the numbers added up, gave him answers.

5

The next day, with a cool voice that matched her white skin, Ms. Daniels read a story about a house that was in the country until the city came and built itself around it. The house grew so sad it had to be moved to the country again. Gregory raised his head off his folded arms to look at the pictures, and at Ms. Daniels twirling a strand of long red hair.

Gregory couldn't believe that she was reading a little kids' book and letting them lie on the floor. At St. John's, no one ever read them anything aloud, especially books with pictures, and they'd sat all day in desks.

At the end, Ms. Daniels asked everyone to sit

up and talk about the house. Some people thought the city would come again to surround it. It would have to be moved again. Matt said that the house might get too shaky from being moved and would fall down.

Like us, Joey, Gregory whispered silently. *Like the way we're moving.*

"I've set out paints and crayons, colored pencils and oil pastels. Each table has large sheets of white paper. I'd like to see the house that *you* live in."

Again, Gregory couldn't believe she was asking them to do such a baby thing.

As though she knew what he was thinking, Ms. Daniels said, "I'm sure you all did this in first grade, but sometimes it helps us to revisit." She turned on soft music.

Gregory wanted to go back to lying on the carpet. He liked feeling the roughness against the whole front of his body.

But the kids were moving toward the tables, and he was left alone in the circle.

Then Ms. Daniels bent down to him, smelling sweet, her red hair close enough to touch. "Gregory, you draw the house you *used* to live in." She knew about the motel, then. How did she know?

He wanted to tell her all about the motel, how the days were slipping away. But she was gone.

Gregory drew the house at Bird Springs. It was made of bits of this and that—pine trees with the bark still on, corrugated tin, and sheets of plywood. He noticed that Joey was drawing the same thing, but that Joey had gotten all the angles just right and had sketched in the textures of the various materials. He wondered what was happening to the house now that they no longer lived in it. Maybe Dad had moved back in after they'd gone. But he couldn't have. Without the sheep, there was no way to make money, no way to live. At the bottom of the page, Gregory wrote: "This was ours."

Only then did he look up and see the houses the other kids were drawing and painting, the windows and doors, the watercolor trees outside. He already knew that no houses in this neighborhood looked that nice.

Gregory folded his hands and waited.

"May I take it?" Ms. Daniels pinned the drawing to the wall with four tacks.

When it was up, Gregory took a deep breath.

Yes, although he had left, he *had* lived in that house. And now he had drawn it as proof, and it hung here in the room with him.

"How come you didn't draw the house you live in now?" Matt asked.

Gregory rolled a colored pencil across the table. "I live in the motel by the school."

"The one by the freeway?"

"Yup."

"That's no motel. That's a shelter. That's for people without houses."

"I have a house. At Bird Springs."

Matt ignored him and asked, "How long you gonna live in the shelter?"

Gregory shrugged. "I dunno. Till my dad comes to get me, I guess."

"Your *dad?*"

"Yeah, I got a dad. Don't you?"

"Nope. At least I ain't never seen him."

"My dad is a warrior," Gregory surprised himself by saying. "He gots a horse called Blackie, and one day when he gets Blackie back he's gonna ride on down and get me."

Matt's blue eyes widened. "Cool! Maybe he could take me, too."

"Maybe." It would be fun to show Matt the fort on the wash, the cave in the cliff.

Joey elbowed Gregory hard in the ribs.

"If that place, Bird Springs, is so great, how come you're here?"

"It didn't rain anymore."

"So? It don't rain here, neither. We still got water."

"It's different on the reservation."

"At least at that shelter place you got water."

Gregory thought of how the water flowed, warm and rusty, into the motel bathtub. At Bird Springs, they'd hauled water from the well at Three Points. Dad had pulled the truck up next to the pump spout and filled the barrels. Back at the house, he'd unloaded the barrels onto the hill above the house. Gravity carried the water into the kitchen sink and into the tin tub for bathing. An outhouse hid in a grove of piñon pines behind the house.

After Dad had left, they'd had to leave, too, because Mom had no way to haul water, no way to get the barrels onto the hill. No way could they stay.

When the rain had stopped, the creek had dried up and so had the storage tanks of water for the livestock. Gregory's cousins Timothy and Susanna, along with their parents and grandmother, had left the reservation, and so had Uncle Felix. "We're headed for Phoenix, maybe Tucson," Uncle Felix had said. "Tucson's smaller and cooler."

After they'd left, the drought went on. Blackie and the sheep had to be sold. Dad had sat by the wood-burning stove on the cool nights, whittling at sticks of cottonwood, then throwing them into the flames. One night he'd driven off, the truck tires popping over the twigs as he backed up. He hadn't returned.

Mom had waited for him, day after day, at the front door, rocking Jeanine, shifting her from one hip to the other. Almost everyone had left Bird Springs but them.

On the third day, Gregory had set off walking for the springs. The little collection of houses was named for that pool where the birds drank. He'd ridden Blackie there before and knew it was a long way. He took a package of saltines and a soda.

He hiked across the flat red land to the mouth of the canyon, then entered it. The canyon narrowed. Gregory had to climb over boulders as he neared the end. Lace ferns and tiny red flowers grew in the rock crevices. There, in the cool dimness, several springs leaked from the rock. As Gregory approached, a flock of birds darted upward into the sky above the steep walls of the canyon.

The springs were all the water that was left. Hardly any rain had fallen for two years. This included the winter snow and the summer monsoons with their forks of lightning and bursts of loud thunder.

In one way, not having rain was a good thing. Gregory didn't need to worry about flash floods.

During the rainy season, the canyon could suddenly fill with a wall of water, a wallawater, that crushed everything in its path.

Gregory recalled the summer day that Uncle Felix had ridden his horse up to the house, bringing the reins up tight so that the horse's hooves made a big cloud of dust as he dug them in.

"Whew! I got stuck in a flash flood," he said to Gregory, climbing down from the horse.

Gregory noticed that sticks were caught in Uncle Felix's long hair. His leather shoes were damp.

"It came at me like a wallawater, right out of nowhere. Sounded like the whole mountain was coming down the creek."

"Couldn't you swim away?"

"Heck, no. Rocks and even trees were coming at me."

"How did you get away?"

"I got soaked with the first wave, then I climbed straight up the cliff." Uncle Felix held out his hands. The fingertips were rubbed raw. "Thank goodness this horse of mine had sense and ran to safety."

Gregory looked around at the sheer walls of the canyon. He should plan an escape route just in case. But it hadn't rained in forever. . . .

He took off his shoes and socks and put his hot feet into the small pool at the base of the rock wall. The water was so cold it burnt his feet. He ate the saltines, drank the soda, then lay back in the damp sand.

Joey arrived that afternoon. Gregory felt him first as a breeze that stayed close instead of passing on. Joey came into gradual focus like the pictures from the Polaroid camera Mr. Flores had at school.

Go away, he said at first. *You're just made up. Only babies make up pretend friends.*

Yet by the time the sun had set behind the high canyon walls, Gregory and Joey were skipping stones across the pool. As they walked out of the canyon, it was Joey's idea to shout their names at the canyon walls and listen for the echo. At the mouth of the canyon, they stood together in silence as the landscape opened before them—red and wild and big.

A week after Dad took off, when the time came to leave Bird Springs, Joey went, too.

Mom laid out three boxes, and Gregory helped her pack their clothes—his, hers, and Jeanine's.

Me, too, Joey had insisted.

So Gregory had laid out an imaginary box, and when Mom wasn't looking, folded imaginary clothes, thinking, *This is so stupid. This is so crazy.* But he couldn't stop himself.

He tucked the folder of Dad's drawings into his own box.

When the boxes were packed, Gregory and Mom tied them up with rope, making handles to carry them with.

"Will we take these?" He touched one of the wool blankets. Woven with zigzaggy Navajo patterns, the blankets had been in the family for a long time.

"Those are too heavy to carry. Besides, it's too hot in the city for those," Mom said.

"The *city*? We're going to the city?" Gregory had never been to a real city. He'd only seen pictures of cities in schoolbooks and on the trading post TV.

"That's the only place for us now," Mom replied. "We'll go to Tucson. Maybe your cousins are there."

Gregory felt a squiggle of excitement. Maybe there would be some fun in the move after all.

It was definitely cold enough in Bird Springs for wool blankets. The late September breeze blew under the front door. Gregory shivered in his flannel shirt, but Mom didn't light the wood-burning stove.

Instead, she washed the pots in the last of the water, dried them, and put them on the shelves.

"We won't take these, either?" Gregory asked.

"Too heavy, hon."

"Why are you cleaning them, then?"

"So that when we come back, everything will be neat."

Jeanine began to cry.

"Rock her, will you?" Mom asked. "Here's her bottle."

Gregory took Jeanine in his arms, sat down on the edge of the bed, and eased the bottle into Jeanine's mouth.

Finally Mom put on her long-sleeved, high-collared velvet blouse and her crinkly velvet skirt. Around her neck, she hung her mother's necklace of lumpy turquoise stones the color of an October sky.

Mom put Jeanine in the stroller, they picked up the boxes, and Gregory pulled the door tight behind them.

Mom snapped on the padlock.

Gregory stood a moment in the clearing in front of the house, memorizing the cabin, the empty sheep pen, Blackie's lonely corral. He took one last deep breath of the piñon pines' sun-baked sweetness.

Going down the rutty dirt road to the highway, Mom pushed Jeanine in the stroller, with Jeanine's box of clothes hanging over the stroller handles.

Gregory carried his own box and Mom's. The ropes bit into his fingers.

Joey carried his suitcase-box, throwing it into the air and catching it.

At the highway, they began to walk on the shoulder of the road. Often, the late summer flowers—yellow clusters on tall gray stalks—blocked their way and they had to walk on the road itself.

After about half an hour, Mr. Atkinson, the white man who owned the trading post, stopped his truck. "Looks like you folks could use a ride."

Mom and Jeanine got in the front, Jeanine on Mom's lap.

Gregory and Joey rode in the truck bed with the stroller and boxes. The September sun, away from the cooling trees, was warm. He glimpsed the house one more time, just below the place where the soft hill changed to rock.

The landscape flashed by, and the breeze blew his hair. High in the mountains above, the golden coins of the aspen leaves clattered together. Above, the blue sky spread over the world.

Joey tilted his head back so that the sun shone full on his face.

Mr. Atkinson dropped them off at the bus stop.

"Thank you," Mom said. "Our relatives will be waiting for us at the other end."

"Have a nice visit." Mr. Atkinson waved and drove off.

"Relatives?" Gregory asked. "Are they really meeting us?" He thought of Timothy and Susanna, Uncle Felix, and Johnny. Or did Mom mean that *Dad* would be meeting them?

Mom pushed the hair off his forehead. "No, no relatives, hon. We might find your cousins, but I don't know. I just didn't want the man to feel sorry for us."

As they waited for the bus, she gave him money to get a ham-and-cheese sandwich from a machine, then went into the bathroom to change Jeanine's diaper.

The bus came, and they piled into the interior, which had gray reclining seats and gray lights on the ceiling. When Gregory looked at Mom, her face was gray, too.

As they coasted down from the high country, the sun coasted down across the sky.

Finally it set. As it slipped out of sight, Gregory wondered if he'd see the same sun ever again. Would it shine just the same in the city?

"We're almost in Tucson," Mom said, cradling Jeanine, who slept innocently.

Joey slept, his head against Gregory's shoulder.

But Gregory gazed into the city night, expecting to see stars. Instead of being inky black, bursting with points of light, the sky was pale pink.

Ahead he saw so many lights it looked as if the stars had fallen to earth. Constellation upon constellation lay before him.

Jeanine woke up and blinked at the city lights.

"Do you see where Uncle Felix lives?" Gregory asked.

Mom laughed. "Finding Uncle Felix would be like throwing a pebble into a rushing river and expecting to find it again."

"You mean we won't?"

Mom took his hand. "I doubt it, honey."

"And not Timothy or Susanna, either?"

"This city is very big. Hundreds of thousands of people live here. I don't think we could ever find our family." She let go of his hand and pulled his head onto her shoulder.

Gregory didn't dare ask about Dad. He sank against Mom, feeling like a thrown pebble himself.

"Where will we go in the city?" Gregory asked, looking into the mass of lights.

Mom tapped her pocket, and he heard the rustle

of paper. "I have an address here—a place that takes care of people like us."

Gregory let out a sigh. At least they were headed somewhere definite in that shifting constellation of city stars.

8

"I know where you live," said Matt the next day. "I lived there once, too."

They were making a house out of a small box. Gregory kept his eyes on the window he was cutting.

They sawed out a front door that opened. Matt put a chimney on the roof. They each took a brush.

"How about red?" asked Matt.

"Red is good," Gregory agreed.

Joey was in the corner, his bottom lip pushed out in a pout because there wasn't an extra brush.

"What do you mean, you lived there?"

"Before my mom got rent money. We moved then."

"My mom's gonna get money, too." *Or Dad will come with it,* he thought.

When the house was finished, Ms. Daniels set it on a shelf. "Matt and Gregory," she wrote beside it.

Gregory wasn't sure how he felt about having his name written with Matt's.

Joey turned his chair so that it faced the wall.

Hey, don't be jealous, Gregory said mind-to-mind.

But at the same time, he stared at the miniature home of a red box, at their names written together— not *Joey and Gregory*, but *Matt and Gregory*.

A house. He imagined shrinking himself and living inside the box house.

Down to twenty-six days already.

In science, Mr. Best showed a video about how an iceberg could be floated down from Alaska and melted to provide freshwater. If only an iceberg could be flown to Bird Springs.

After school, Gregory stopped off at the boys' room to comb his hair. Matt and the other boy were right—he needed a haircut. His hair hung shaggy and uneven, just below his shoulders. He tucked in his shirt.

Ms. Daniels had invited him to join the chess club. He had to tell her now.

"Um, miss . . ." He stood with his backpack on the ground in front of him, grasping it by the straps. He needed it to be there, between them.

She turned from the papers she was stacking, a thin bracelet dangling from her pale wrist.

He had all of her attention. "I'm gonna be here less than a month," he said.

"Less than a month?"

"Yeah, that's the limit for staying."

"Oh, yes, the shelter." She reached out her hand as though to touch him, then pulled it back. "After a month, then what?"

"I dunno." Gregory shrugged. "A month unless we get three strikes against us. Then we're out sooner."

"What kind of strikes?"

"Oh, like hopping the fence at night. Or not keeping the kitchen clean."

"But those are such small things. . . ."

"Yup." His shoes pinched his toes.

"Just be careful."

"When we move, maybe we'll live close."

"Let's hope." But she didn't look at him.

"My mom's gonna be finding us a house, soon as she gets a job."

"That's good." Ms. Daniels stared down at her papers.

To make her feel better, Gregory brought out his three new Batmen.

They'd gotten a little crumpled, but she spread them smooth on the table with her long fingers.

"The ones with the wings are extra special," he told her.

"I can see that. May I put them up in the room?"

Gregory rocked from one foot to the other. If he gave her the Batmen, part of himself would be gone. Or saved here in this room. Saved here with her.

"Okay. But just one."

After Ms. Daniels had stapled the green one to the wall above the art supplies, she unrolled a poster. On it, a boy flew on the back of a huge white goose into a sky as dark blue and filled with stars as nighttime at Bird Springs.

"It's for me?" With his fingertip, he touched the face of the boy, whose hair was long like his own, streaming back in the wind.

Ms. Daniels seemed to be telling him that if he wanted, he could fly wherever he wanted.

"If you like it." She seemed to be saying he was somehow like the magnificent boy. Or could be.

"But I got no place for it. They don't let us put anything on the walls of our room."

"Save it until you have a home," Ms. Daniels said, as though she were sure that one day he would.

That night, Mom came home wearing a pair of plain brown pants and a white blouse that buttoned up the front. From a bag, she pulled out her velvet Navajo clothing. As she hung the skirt and blouse carefully in the closet, she said, "Mr. Hass says I'll never get work if I go around looking like an Indian."

That might be true, Gregory thought. He hadn't seen anyone dressed in velvet. He thought of Ms. Daniels in her flowing dresses.

"What about Grandma's necklace?" he asked. "You aren't going to wear that, either?"

"I've hidden it somewhere safe."

"Where?"

She shook her head and closed the closet door. "It's more of a secret if only I know."

After school the next day, Gregory pulled the curtains and lay down on the bed.

Someone knocked. Gregory sat up. Should he answer? Who could it be? It might be Dad. His blood ran faster.

"Greg, it's me, it's me. Surprise!" Matt called.

Gregory slid off the bed, pulling the thin cover with him.

He opened the door, and Matt stood there with two slingshots in his hands.

"Me go hunting." Matt held up the slingshot. "Red man show how."

Joey yanked on Gregory's arm, as though to pull him back to the bed.

Gregory stepped outside and closed the door behind him, shutting Joey inside.

The shelter had such strict rules. "Who let you in?" he asked.

"No one. I just came. We used to live over there, across the pool. In number"—Matt squinted—"in number nine. Until they kicked us out. You know the three-strike thing. Well, we got it. Then somehow my mom got money together to rent us a house."

Gregory scuffed at the peeling paint on the sidewalk with his toe. "How'd ya get the strikes?" He didn't know if he wanted to find out or not. But he couldn't help asking.

Matt slipped one slingshot into each back pocket and began to explain with his hands. "The first strike was I knocked out a light with my slingshot. The second was—let me remember—oh, yeah, my brother, Ricky, he climbed the fence by the pool and tried to get in. And last of all, my mom snuck in her boyfriend."

"And Mr. Hass still lets you visit?" Gregory asked.

"Well, this is the first time I've tried. I thought it would be cool to surprise you, ya know?"

Gregory looked around. He didn't see Mr. Hass anywhere. He didn't know which would be worse— to hide Matt inside the room or to be out here in the open with him. Would Matt's visit be a strike against Gregory's family?

"Hey, dude. I know a place where there's still tadpoles. We can catch 'em in a old water bottle."

Gregory put his hand to his eyes against the sun and looked up at Matt. He didn't know what to say. He should be at home where he had promised to be, doing homework. Close to Jeanine in day care in case she needed him. Close to Joey. Here in case Mom came home from her job hunt.

"Come on, man," Matt insisted.

"Just for a little while then." Gregory opened the door a crack so that Joey could slip out and come along, too, then banged the door and locked it.

No clouds anywhere.

Joey stepped on the back of Gregory's shoe, giving him a flat tire.

Matt led the way across the street and over a weedy vacant lot to a drainage ditch. At the bottom of the ditch, there was water the color of the hot cinnamon cocoa Mom made when the mornings got cold and wind snapped the air.

Matt slid down standing up, like he was riding a big brown wave. Rocks cascaded around his ankles.

Gregory looked for a different way to get down. There was none. He sat down and scooted on his rear.

"Check out your pants!" Matt pointed and laughed.

Gregory slapped his jeans, and dust billowed around him.

Joey laughed, too, along with Matt.

"Well, like I said, here's the frog babies," said Matt.

They leaned over the muddy water to see the tadpoles, swimming with their wavy tails.

"At Bird Springs, where I used to live, there was lots of tadpoles that filled up the wash after it rained."

"I thought you never got no rain up there."

"Well, sometimes a little." Gregory closed his eyes and recalled how at night he fell asleep to the frogs' throaty calls.

"Oh! I forgot the water bottle. I'll have to use my hands." Matt scooped up a tadpole.

Gregory got hold of one, too. It swam in the little pool in his palm. When the water drained out between his fingers, he released the tadpole into the puddle.

But Matt set his on a rock. It flipped back and forth.

"It needs wa—" Gregory started to say.

"Okay, okay. I'll put it back in a minute."

Gregory watched the tadpole struggling to breathe the air. It needed water. The same way that everything at Bird Springs needed water. He stood up. He wanted to get out of there. His lungs clenched so he couldn't get a breath.

"Where ya going, Greg?" Matt called after him. "I put it back already! Stay and I'll just catch 'em and let 'em go. I swear!"

But Gregory had already stumbled to the top. He crossed the vacant lot, then the street. He should have known that Matt was a jerk. Now he knew why Matt was in Ms. Daniels's class.

Joey pounded ahead.

Without even glancing around for Mr. Hass, Gregory entered the shelter, walked quickly past the dry pool, and unlocked his door.

Gradually, he felt Joey come into sharp focus. The two sat side by side on the edge of the bed.

When Gregory's breathing returned to normal, he got the bag of marbles from under the bed. He smoothed the bedspread, then drew a circle in the thin cotton with his fingertip. He put the marbles in the middle of the circle, gave himself and Joey each a jumbo size, and invited Joey to take the first turn.

A knock came on the door. It might be Dad. Or Mr. Hass. Gregory cocked his ear and listened.

Joey held his breath, too.

Gregory heard Matt's scuffing feet. He didn't open up.

When the sun glowed rosy through the white curtains, Mom came in, wearing her brown pants and white blouse, carrying the box from the Food Bank with Jeanine's box of formula on top.

Gregory wanted to tell her about Matt and the way he'd come into the shelter without being stopped. Even with three strikes against him. He wanted to share about the tadpole Matt had almost killed by keeping it out of the water.

But when he looked at her, he understood that she couldn't take any bad news, that the job hunt had not gone well. "D'ja get work?" he asked.

She sat down on the edge of the bed, removed one of her new black shoes, and began to massage her foot. "I got a week of temporary work, honey. Cleaning a bank. It's at night, so you'll have to take Jeanine after the day care closes." She looked up at him. "I know it's tough, hon. But if we hang in there, we'll be fine."

"Will you make enough to get us a house?"

Mom laughed quickly and began to tug at her toes one at a time, popping the knuckles.

"My friend used to live here. His mom got money to rent a house," Gregory said.

"That's good," Mom said. She walked over to the food and wrapped the greenish bananas in a bag to ripen. "Let's take this food to the fridge." She handed him a gallon of milk and tucked the block of cheese under his arm.

In the kitchen, they had to wait for a burner. The old lady named Martina was using one. Another didn't work, and the big lady with the girls who always dressed in fluffy party dresses cooked on the last two. The girls played hopscotch outside, and Gregory heard the click of their rocks falling on the cement path.

When Martina pulled her canned soup off the burner, Mom heated up the beans and rice from the Tupperware marked with their name.

"Just for tonight, let's get Jeanine later. I'm so tired," Mom said, handing Gregory his plate and glass of milk. They found a spot on a curb by the gravel pathway. Between bites, Gregory slapped at mosquitoes.

Mr. Hass had said that the patio tables and chairs had walked off long ago. When he'd seen Gregory's face twist up, he'd touched him lightly on the top of his head. "Not really, little guy, I know. Someone stole them."

After they'd washed the plates and forks in the sink and put them on the shelf, they went next door to get Jeanine.

Usually, Bertha, the evening caregiver, would gather up Jeanine and snuggle her and pretend to be sad to give her back to Mom. But tonight she left Jeanine in her stroller. She handed Mom the sign-out book without a smile. "I know when you came home," she said. "You dumped her here a extra forty-five minutes."

Gregory stood closer to Mom, as though his body could become part of hers like before he'd been born. He didn't want Bertha's eyes to land on him.

"But . . ." Mom spread her hands.

"But nothing, ma'am. Rules is rules. I ain't gonna be responsible. When Mr. Hass finds out that you was back forty-five minutes and didn't come for your baby, that's a strike."

Mom said nothing, but her hand was shaking as she signed the book that Bertha held still for her in the air.

Gregory tucked Jeanine's blanket tight around her even though it was still hot as hot outside. Maybe Bertha would tell Mr. Hass about Matt's visit. Maybe she'd been peeking through the curtains and had seen the blond visitor at number 3. Not just a visitor but a person who had struck out.

Strike one had come upon them so quickly. The visit would be strike two. Mom should know so she could plan the next thing. But Gregory couldn't tell her, just couldn't.

When they got back in and closed the door, Mom sat down on the chair with Jeanine in her lap. She fed her the bottle of formula but didn't baby talk to her or tickle her tummy. She looked across the room at nothing.

"Dad should come be with us," Gregory said.

Mom spread one hand wide. "How could he know where we are?"

"He could hire a detective to find us."

Mom laughed, but not like she thought anything was funny. Then she said, "Come here, honey." With one arm still around Jeanine, she pulled Gregory close and kissed his cheek.

Gregory lay back on the bed, his feet still touching the floor. In his daydreams, Dad came for them in the truck, which was tuned up and running good. It didn't have the oil leak anymore. The headlight on the passenger side was fixed. They would all climb in, Jeanine on Mom's lap. The whole way, Gregory's body would be next to Dad's, getting to know Dad all over again.

As they drove with the windows open, the temperature would drop and drop until they arrived at Bird Springs, the air so sweet and cold Gregory imagined lapping it up like ice cream. Blackie would be neighing softly in the corral.

And there at last—the house. Lit by the bare bulb, by the fire in the woodstove, standing against the darkness, it was a place that could hold them all. Gregory would run out of the truck, passing underneath billions of stars.

The next day before class, Matt handed Gregory a little rock. "Sorry."

The rock looked like a piece of butterscotch, tannish and clear. In Bird Springs, by the back door, Gregory had a collection of rocks. He wondered if the pile was still there—the oval ones, the striped ones, those with the crystals jagged on the insides. He rubbed his finger over Matt's rock. He thought of the tadpole.

Joey thought of the tadpole, too. *Give it back,* he insisted.

Gregory began to put the rock in his pocket instead. He didn't look at Joey.

"Hey, Greg, don't *steal* it," said Matt loudly.

Gregory handed the rock back to Matt. The guy was so weird.

"Can I come over today? I promise I won't do nothing wrong," Matt asked.

"I don't think so. I mean, we got a strike last night. If Mr. Hass—"

"Oh, I know him. He likes me. It's the rest of my family he don't like. A strike for what?"

"For leaving my baby sister too long at day care."

Matt snorted. "Those jerks. They'll think up anything to get you out of there."

Ms. Daniels led them on an imaginary journey. A blue ocean. A red rowboat. Crossing to an island, smelling the salty air, hearing the gulls. The island got closer and closer. They landed and felt white sand underfoot. A trail led into a green jungle. They climbed until they came to a cliff and a cave within the cliff. Entering the cave, they found a hallway. Along the hall were doors. "Imagine what's inside," Ms. Daniels commanded softly.

It could be a place they remembered, a place they'd forgotten, a new place, an old place, inside or outside. "Now unlock your door and look. What's behind it? When you have seen all there is to see, open your eyes."

Gregory opened his right away. He reached for the paper and the nearest crayons. He quickly drew three doors. But he didn't open them. They were locked against him. He sat back, finished, hoping that Ms. Daniels would tell him to get a book from the shelf and read.

"I don't like my picture," he heard Matt telling Ms. Daniels.

Gregory watched her bend over Matt's shoulder, spreading her hands onto the table, leaning close. "Tell me about it anyway."

"These here are the three demons." Matt pointed to black shapes. "And this is a guy all bloody, with knives stabbing him."

Ms. Daniels didn't say anything. She just hovered over Matt, looking and looking at what he'd drawn.

Finally she came to Gregory and his three doors. "What's behind them?" she asked.

Gregory shrugged.

"There must be *something*."

He shrugged again.

"What's inside the doors, Gregory?"

"Nothing, miss. They're locked." He wouldn't look. No way.

She moved on then, leaving the drawing in front of him. He'd failed her. He made his hands into fists under the table.

She went on to Tessie's drawing of a bedroom with bunk beds and a CD player on a chest of drawers. All fake, Gregory thought. Bedrooms like that were only in books and on TV.

Ms. Daniels hadn't told him to start reading. He wanted to look away from the doors but couldn't. What did Ms. Daniels want him to understand? He already knew that he was locked out of Bird Springs. He'd closed the door and Mom had padlocked it.

There was nothing to understand, he insisted to himself. He knew every inch of that cabin.

Twenty-five days. After that, there might be no more doors.

Ms. Daniels was pointing to other kids' papers and asking questions. Some kids had answers.

Suddenly she was behind him again, bending over him, sweet smelling and fresh, wanting to know everything. She put her fingertip on the first door. "I think that behind here is something that you don't want to think about."

She wouldn't leave until he said something. He couldn't fail her again. "Behind that," he said, closing his eyes, "was when Johnny was supposed to have his birthday party. But he got sick and we couldn't celebrate. Not any of us."

"Hmm," Ms. Daniels said. "And this door?" She put her finger on the middle one. Her voice was so soft, sweet as pancake syrup. He would tell her whatever she wanted to know.

But he felt crampy in his heart area. "That one. Huh." What made him uncomfortable to think of? "That was when Blackie tripped and hurt his foot. He couldn't walk around for a whole week."

"And the last one, Gregory?"

He looked at the clock. Ten minutes left.

"The last one, Gregory." Ms. Daniels wouldn't give up.

A fist closed over his heart. He squeezed his eyes closed. "Not that door, miss. Please."

She didn't say anything. But she didn't leave.

And suddenly he saw behind it. Once again, Jeanine had cried too much. Once again, Dad had pushed Mom. He'd pushed her down. With Jeanine in her arms. He'd pushed.

Gregory couldn't open his eyes.

Ms. Daniels put both hands on his shoulders and left them there until the bell rang.

In the morning, just as he rounded the corner on the way to Mr. Best's class, Gregory thought he saw—yes, he did—an old blue pickup cruising slowly past the school. He held his hand to his forehead against the sun. The truck disappeared in a blur of sunshine.

He ran to the fence. Dad had come.

Gregory hung on the chain-link fence so hard that the wire made grooves in his fingers. Yet the pickup didn't return.

"Please, mister," he said as Mr. Best opened the classroom door, "I saw my dad's blue pickup drive by. I want to stay out and watch for it."

Mr. Best waited until the class had gone inside. Then he said, "I can't let you be out here alone. Come inside." With one hand, he adjusted the bow tie at his neck. With the other, he shut the door.

Gregory stared at the closed door. He thought of flinging it open and running outside the fence in spite of Mr. Best. But if Mr. Hass found out, that might turn into a strike. And besides, Dad would wait for him. Dad wouldn't give up.

All through class, he couldn't concentrate. Every little bit of him felt crazy to be outside hanging on the fence.

"Gregory," Mr. Best says quietly. "There's a man in the office to see you. It may be your father."

Gregory catches his breath and traps a knot of happiness in his throat. He leaves the classroom without even getting a pass. Dashing across the green lawn, he startles the crows. He pushes open the double doors of the office.

There stands Dad—his cowboy boots, his big hat, his jewelry, his thick, long braid hanging down the back of his coat.

Gregory runs to him and hugs him with both arms, pressing his face against Dad's leather jacket, smudged with dirt, smelling smoky, like the inside of the house at Bird Springs.

"Had a heck of a time finding you, son." Dad sits

down in one of the blue plastic chairs and looks up.
"You've gotten so tall. . . ."

Gregory smells the sage on him. A song winds in
and out of his heart to the rhythm of Blackie's gallop.

"Gregory," said Mr. Best, "time to think about nega-
tive fractions."

Gregory pretended to focus on his book filled
with minus signs, but his heart was still galloping.

At the springs hidden in the cliff, flocks of
birds flew in and out of the yellow trees. When he
got to Bird Springs, he would lean down and push
aside the clumpy ferns. He would wash his face in
the clear water that burbled out of the rocks. And
then he would drink until all his thirsty places were
satisfied.

"What ya lookin' for?" Matt asked during lunch
break.

"My dad's blue pickup. It's got a big dent in the
front part."

"I thought you said he was coming on a horse."

"Horse, truck, it doesn't matter! This way he can
get my whole family."

"And me, too," said Matt. "I can ride in the

back." He stretched out his arms as though he were lying in a truck bed.

Yes, it would be fun to have Matt. He could help with the sheep.

Would Dad drive back the same way, by the underpass? Or had he circled the neighborhood? Would he come from the direction of the tire shop? A thousand pinwheels turned inside Gregory, all going in different directions.

Surely Dad wouldn't pass by just *once*. Maybe he'd circled a lot of times while Gregory was inside all morning, but he'd be back.

"I saw Dad's truck today," Gregory told Mom that evening. They sat with Jeanine in the courtyard, eating refried beans with crackers and cheese.

Mom looked up quickly, a bite of beans balanced on her cracker. "Where?"

"By the school. He was looking for me."

Mom still hadn't put the cracker in her mouth. Her hand shook so that the beans fell off. "Did you actually see your dad inside the truck?"

Gregory picked up a slice of cheese. "It was moving away. I couldn't tell for sure." The halo of light had kept him from seeing.

"There's lots of trucks that look like that one."
Mom finally put the cracker in her mouth.

"But I had a *feeling*. . . ."

Mom chewed and swallowed, then said, "Feelings aren't always the truth, hon. I'd be very, very surprised if that was your dad's truck."

Just then, Jeanine leaned up from her stroller and pointed her finger in the air.

"See, she's pointing to where Dad is," Gregory said.

Mom laughed. "I think it was that bird that got her attention."

Gregory looked up at the bird perched on the Coke machine. Dad hadn't found them after all. He wished Mom wouldn't act so relieved.

That night after Mom had gone to clean the bank, Gregory made sure that Jeanine's bottle was full, then slipped her into the stroller. "Just a little ride," he said when she looked up at him.

Instead of wheeling Jeanine by Mr. Hass's office, Gregory took her to a hole in the oleander hedge. He had to twist and turn the stroller to get it through. He hoped that none of the poison rubbed off on Jeanine.

"We'll find him," he reassured her when they were out on the sidewalk behind the shelter. With Dad so close, it hardly mattered that Mr. Hass might learn they'd gone.

He wheeled the stroller over the cracked sidewalks and lifted it up and down the curbs. With not much traffic, it was easy to inspect the streets for Dad's blue pickup.

Jeanine began to fuss. She threw her bottle onto the sidewalk, and it bounced into the gutter. Gregory picked it up, then jostled her back and forth as he pushed the stroller. She had to stay quiet.

What if Dad had given up and gone? Maybe one quick little look had been enough for him.

A carnival was being set up by the shopping center. Gregory edged close to the dirt lot to watch. Sometimes carnivals came to the town near Bird Springs, but he'd never seen the big metal arms of the Ferris wheel getting lifted into place, nor the merry-go-round animals stacked together against a truck, separated from the carousel. Only the hot-dog stand was ready, its lights on, the good smells drifting into the night.

Maybe Dad would have enough money to bring

them all here, even Matt. Gregory crouched down beside Jeanine and whispered in her tiny ear, "When we find Dad, he'll buy us sticky pink stuff called cotton candy. Unless you're too scared, we'll ride that ride over there. If we ask the guy, he can make it go extra fast."

A hot breeze rustled by, and Gregory imagined riding in the big striped bowl of the Tilt-A-Whirl, almost bumping into the other bowls of shrieking, laughing people, spinning faster and faster, until all the bad times were spun away.

He imagined himself riding up and up in a cherry red basket on the Ferris wheel.

And yet, pushing Jeanine back to the shelter, he thought that Mom was probably right. There *were* a lot of blue trucks that looked like Dad's.

He remembered, too, what he'd seen behind the painted door. When Ms. Daniels had pressed him, he'd seen it. As the stroller bumped over the dirt sidewalk with its shards of glass and loose pebbles, Gregory once again felt himself hiding, night after night, behind the woodstove, the sparks popping inside the black iron, Mom silent, even Jeanine silent, as Dad had stood over them.

(13)

Matt walked with Gregory to the shelter after school. "What happened with your dad?" he asked. "The blue truck?"

Gregory scuffed at a rock. "I guess it wasn't his."

"But you said . . ."

"It just looked like it was."

The whole way, Joey kept pestering Gregory, saying that being with Matt would only get them in trouble.

Worrywart, Gregory finally said.

He thought of stopping by the office to tell Mr. Hass that Matt was visiting. But Matt was already leading him around the back way, through the hole in the oleander hedge.

Mom was sleeping with the pillow over her eyes

when Gregory opened the door. On the chair lay a big note: J IS IN DAY CARE. SHE CAN STAY THERE.

Gregory shut the door quickly and put his finger over his lips. "Not here," he whispered.

"I know a cool place to go to then," Matt said.

"Where's that?" Gregory kept one hand on the doorknob.

"It's a secret."

Gregory let go of the knob. If he went inside, he'd have to be super quiet. Mom would be better off if he left her in peace.

On the way to Matt's secret place, they found an abandoned shopping cart. They took turns pushing, first with one of them inside, then the other. Gregory wondered if Matt felt Joey's extra weight in the cart, then laughed at the idea. *Don't get carried away.*

When Gregory and Joey pushed Matt, Joey made the cart fall off the curb.

Still no clouds, not even a wisp.

"Here." Matt gestured from the cart.

Gregory braked by putting his sneaker against one of the back wheels. "Where?"

Matt hopped out and crouched down near an opening in the curb. He began to wiggle his body down into the slit. "Don't worry. It gets bigger."

Matt disappeared.

Gregory heard Matt's voice, hollow and echoing from someplace underneath the sidewalk. He sat down and put his legs into the narrow opening. He felt Matt pull on his feet, helping him down.

No way, José, said Joey.

Yet Gregory felt Joey slip in beside him. He even thought he heard Joey say, *Awesome!* as they first landed on a platform above a tunnel, then hopped on down.

"Look," said Matt. He pointed the beam from a tiny penlight ahead into the tunnel. "I always carry this because I come down here a lot."

Gregory felt a layer of mud underfoot. The tunnel was squarish and straight. "What's it for?"

"For when it rains. The water runs into the streets and down here. I forgot you come from that place where they ain't got no streets."

Gregory imagined rain coming and the tunnel filling with water up to the top.

Joey pulled on his sleeve, trying to turn him back toward the opening.

"Don't worry. It don't rain, right? Like never. That's why you're down here from your mountain,"

Matt said, turning the beam of the penlight against the walls of the tunnel. The beam shone on soda cans and other trash in the mud.

He turned off the beam. The blackness was like a cool blanket, thicker even than the darkness at Bird Springs when there was no moon.

Gregory wasn't sure about going down the tunnel after all.

Matt turned the penlight back on and began to walk.

Gregory followed, not wanting to be left in the darkness with only Joey. Matt's penlight shone far ahead, mostly lighting the ceiling. Gregory felt his way by running his hand against one side of the tunnel. The cold concrete chewed at his fingertips.

The tunnel continued in a straight line. Once, it angled sharply and Gregory almost tripped over a pile of garbage.

This place is no fun at all, said Joey.

"We're right under school now," said Matt. He shone the light up toward an opening. It was like the first opening they'd crawled through except that a grating covered this one. It was the grate that Gregory had noticed on his first day.

"That thing can be lifted out." Matt gestured with the penlight.

"Should we go up?" asked Gregory. The tunnel was making him shiver and sweat at the same time.

"Why not?" said Matt.

Gregory locked his hands together, and first Matt, then Joey, stepped into them and up onto the little platform below the opening.

Then Matt and Joey leaned down and pulled Gregory up by his arms.

They peered through the crisscross bars of the grate and saw the grass of the playground, neat and green in spite of how messy and dry the rest of the neighborhood was. Gregory was surprised that it was still daylight.

"Darn," said Matt. "The lawn mower guys are here."

Gregory looked in the direction Matt was pointing. He saw the mower making a big circle at the edge of the grass and then heard its roar.

Five black crows strutted across the lawn.

Joey refused to look out. He hunched down in a corner and put his face on his knees.

"The guy's gonna make littler and littler circles until he's at the very middle of the playground. I know 'cause I seen him do it before. It takes forever."

"Maybe we can come back another time," said Gregory.

"Yeah, explore it when no one is here," said Matt. "I never been in the tunnel at night. We could sneak into our classroom. See what Ms. Daniels has written down about us."

"About how screwed up we are?" Gregory joked.

They both laughed and watched some more. The guy stopped the mower after two more circles. He took out a soda and popped the lid. Gregory heard the whish of the bubbly gas. He imagined the sharp bite of soda in his mouth and wished he had some.

Matt dropped down from the platform again, shining his penlight back and forth in the tunnel. "Darn. I don't remember which way we came."

Gregory looked, too, as the beam swept back and forth, this way and that. Was it his imagination, or was the light yellower and dimmer than it had been earlier?

That way, said Joey, pointing to the right.

But Matt turned the light to the left.

Gregory skinned his palm as he slid from the platform down into the tunnel.

Nothing looked familiar as they walked. Or rather, everything did. Gregory had lost all sense of direction. He felt Joey's hot breath on the back of his neck. The canyon of Bird Springs had been a sort of tunnel. But the canyon had opened to the sky and had never had this trapping feeling. Matt would enjoy exploring that canyon with him. If they ever got out of here.

"This way," Matt said finally. His voice echoed, "**this way**, this way, this way," like Gregory's voice echoing in the canyon. Matt beamed his penlight, which was definitely way yellower, way dimmer, toward another opening.

This time Matt helped Gregory out first. Gregory stepped into the delicate step formed by Matt's interlocked fingers and then pulled himself onto the platform.

Joey was quick and got up before Matt released his hands.

Gregory leaned down and grabbed Matt's forearms to yank him to the platform. When he turned to look out the opening, the sky was dark. The slit seemed to be in the curbing of a busy street. He was eye level with hundreds of moving tires.

"This will be tricky," said Gregory.

Told you we went the wrong way, said Joey. His voice sounded whiny.

"We'll wait till the light turns red," said Matt.

Exhaust fumes blew into their faces. Gregory pulled his shirtsleeve out long and covered his face.

Now! shouted Joey, and crawled out.

Gregory scrambled after him, and then Matt. Gregory grabbed Matt's penlight off the pavement before it could roll back down.

The three of them scooted onto the sidewalk and sat down for a moment so no one would suspect they'd come out of the tunnel. Joey had torn the knee of his pants.

"Guess we went the wrong way," said Matt. "I never been out of this opening before. Look, there's the Cash 'n' Save."

Cash 'n' Save was where people cashed their checks, if they had any. The neon glared against the night sky. Mom had cashed a check in there once and complained that the guy kept too much of it.

Mom. Gregory stood up. Mom would be awake now, wondering where he was.

Now you've really blown it, muttered Joey.

"I gotta get back. I'm supposed to babysit my sister."

Matt walked with him part of the way, turning back at the drainage ditch full of tadpoles.

When Gregory got closer, he saw floodlights turned on at the shelter.

Mr. Hass was talking to three policemen. Mom stood nearby with Jeanine on her hip.

Gregory began to run. He'd been gone too long. He hadn't meant to leave. Not for so long.

But then he stopped. What if the police took him to jail? He knew that being in the tunnel was probably dangerous, but what if it was against the law? He crouched down behind a bush. Maybe Mom would go to jail, too, for not watching him. Who would take care of Jeanine?

No matter what, this would be strike two.

Then Gregory remembered Matt's secret entry

around the back. Maybe he could sneak in and pretend he'd been in the room all along.

Still crouched down, he moved to where the bush ended and the oleander hedge began. He scooted across the gap between them. The hedge ran the length of the motel. As Gregory passed his bathroom window opposite the front door, he wondered if somehow he could pry the window open. But even if he could, the opening was way too small for him.

He continued on to the break behind the swimming pool. From here, he could run quickly down the row of doors to his own.

Just as he set foot on the sidewalk, the floodlight caught him. Gregory shut his eyes at first, then opened them, shielding his face from the light with his hand.

"Is that the boy, ma'am?" asked a man from across the courtyard.

"Gregory!" It was Mom calling him.

But how could he go to her? He wanted to slink back into the hedge, even though it was poisonous. He'd never tried to trick anyone before!

Mom came to him. She hugged him so tight

against her, pressing her head against his collar-bone, that Jeanine got squeezed and began to cry. Mom cried, too, then pushed him away a little so that she could look at his face. "I was so worried! Where have you been? I was due at work an hour ago!"

"With my friend." He hoped Mom couldn't see how dirty he was.

"With your *friend*, sonny?" Mr. Hass said so loudly that Gregory grabbed Mom's arm.

Gregory nodded. He sensed the policemen in their blue uniforms gathering around him.

"Your mother may have lost her job because of you," Mr. Hass continued. He sounded so mad that Gregory thought he'd get taken to jail for sure.

But then the policemen backed away, the gravel scrunching under their boots. When Gregory heard them getting into their cars, he took a deep breath.

"I'll call a taxi," Mr. Hass said. "Buses don't run after dark."

"But that will cost—" Mom objected.

"Better than losing your job, ma'am."

Gregory and Mom stood in silence, waiting for Mr. Hass to call the taxi, then waiting along with

Mr. Hass for the taxi to come. Gregory rocked from one foot to the other.

When the yellow cab pulled close to the curb, Mom handed Jeanine to Gregory, then slid into the dark interior.

Jeanine wailed and reached out to Mom.

Gregory had to grip her tight as the taxi drove off.

"You've got your hands full with your little sister," said Mr. Hass. "That should keep you out of trouble, son. You don't want a third strike."

Back in the room, Jeanine screamed and screamed, even though Gregory walked her and sang "Twinkle, Twinkle, Little Star."

Now they had two strikes. Maybe Jeanine's screaming would get them strike three. Or Bertha, the caregiver, might still tell Mr. Hass that Matt had visited with no permission and would get them struck out.

Told you so, whispered Joey.

"Stop!" Gregory said out loud. From being a comfort, Joey had gone to being a pest.

Finally, when the clock said 11:35, Jeanine collapsed into sleep, breathing softly. Gregory slipped

did they
aken care

he woke
comfort
they had

en him.
d on the
d never

n he'd

r, the
e.
i

her crib. He shook out

cept for the motel light
ns.

y'd *have* to find Dad. But
without even saying good-
to see them, even when he
d them. Now that he didn't
ssibly come? Would he even
?

at the pale orange glow of the
Dad was gone, he was the man
y got kicked out of the shelter, it
m to find a place for all of them.
o idea how to do that. He clasped
her. They felt bony and hollow.

r the school, he'd seen people with
hey owned in a shopping cart. Maybe
would put him and Jeanine somewhere
Mom be on the street like that, pushing a
m one corner to another, her Navajo clothes
g.

st been having a little fun with Matt. If it
Jeanine, Mom could have gone to work

and trusted that he'd be home later. Wh
have to have a stupid baby who had to be
of all the time?

He turned on the light. He didn't care i
Jeanine. If she did wake up, he wouldn't
her. He'd let her scream. It was her fault
two strikes. And Mom blamed *him* now.

He found the poster Ms. Daniels had gi
He would never fly free like the boy perche
goose. Nor would he ever go home. He wou
have a wall of his own to hang the poster on

He'd be leaving Ms. Daniels sooner th
feared. And he hadn't even found Dad.

He began to tear at the edges of the poste
ripped a straight line to the boy's happy fa
held the face in his palm for a moment, then
it into tiny pieces.

15

de. Do you want to know how mad Mr.
′ at me?" Gregory said at lunch.

tten about that already." Matt
e slice, nibbling down to the

milk carton, the waxy
police, Matt. They
dn't? What if they
way?"

s works out,

urbled

and
then,"

Mr. Hass,
"One more

egory held the
ck heavy on his

Walking into the shelter, Gregory spotted Mr. Hass sweeping the walk. If only there were another way in. He didn't want to see Mr. Hass after last night.

But there was no other entry, so Gregory marched along the path until he met Mr. Hass.

"You okay, son?" Mr. Hass asked, leaning on the broom so that the straw fanned onto the concrete. "No problems at school?"

"None at all, sir."

"Good. I got something for you then." Mr. Hass crooked the broom in his elbow, took out his wallet and extracted a coupon.

Gregory read: ONE FREE HAIRCUT.

"Cecilia's around the corner—red, white, blue barber pole. She donates every now and Mr. Hass explained.

"Thank you, sir."

"You got to be careful, son," said tucking the wallet back into his pocket chance."

"I know, sir."

As he walked to the room, G coupon in one hand, his backpa

shoulder. Now he could look nice. Never get teased again.

But when he reached the doorstep, he realized he didn't know what kind of haircut he wanted: just a trim so he could keep being like Dad, or a short, regular white-boy cut.

There's a carnival at the shopping center," Gregory said to Mom on Saturday. "You could take me and Jeanine."

Mom was braiding her hair, head turned to one side, fingers busily twisting the strands this way and that. "I have to work today, hon. Cleaning the office, remember?" She slipped a rubber band over the end of the braid.

He looked down at the blue carpet with ridges and hollows just like real land.

Mom reached up and laid her hands on his shoulders. "Me working is good news, Gregory, not bad," she said. "We'll have more money this week."

"Enough for a house?"

She sighed. "Not quite."

"Almost?" He wanted her to look up into his eyes, but now it was she who looked down at the blue rug.

"We'll see." She gave his shoulders a squeeze. "You've been a hero, honey."

He sat down at the table, opened his science book, and read about how the human body has lots of water in it. From the corner of his eye, he saw Mom go into the bathroom, lift the lid of the toilet tank, and peer inside. What could she be looking for?

Mom set the lid straight with a clunk.

After she'd left, pushing Jeanine's stroller over the threshold and across the courtyard to the day care, Gregory lifted the tank lid himself. There, next to a rubber ring and a loose chain, he saw Grandma's necklace, like a pirate's treasure, the turquoise shining extra bright in the clear water. So that was where she'd been keeping it. Gregory replaced the tank lid.

He lay down on the bed and imagined the carnival, imagined riding a bright red basket high up into the air. He wondered if he'd be scared.

Maybe Mom would take him to the carnival tonight after she got home.

Gregory heard a crash against the window, then Matt's voice, low and husky: "Hey, Greg! Mr. Hass is out front, so I couldn't come in."

Gregory realized that Matt had thrown a pebble against the frosted glass of the bathroom window. Carefully, he cranked it open. He hoped that Matt saw that he was opening up and wouldn't throw anything else.

Matt stood below, shading his blue eyes with his hand. "Hey, it's a great tunnel day. We can go farther. I know how now."

Gregory wanted to say, *Hey, yeah!* and lace up his sneakers ready to go, but Joey was whispering, *Don't listen to him.* Mom would never take them to the carnival if anything bad happened. And no way should he risk strike three.

"Not today."

"But why not? Is it 'cause we almost got lost?"

"No. I just don't wanna. It was kind of fun but not all the way fun."

"I'm getting a new battery for my light."

"It's not that."

"Well, if you change your mind, meet me at noon next to the opening at school. I'm going down right after the skateboarding on TV."

"You shouldn't go in the tunnel alone."

"But I do. I'm always okay."

"See ya, then," Gregory said, beginning to crank the window closed.

"You're just scared," Matt said suddenly.

"Am not."

"Are too. I thought you Indian guys was all brave and all. You're a big chicken. I bet your dad is a big chicken, too."

"Is not!" Gregory had never punched anyone, but now he wanted to. He opened the window wider.

"Oh, look at you being a big shot from inside your house. I mean, your room," Matt taunted.

Gregory looked down for something to throw at Matt. All he found was a bar of soap. He picked it up but when he hurled it it slipped between his fingers and fell on the ground.

"That's supposed to *hurt* me?" Matt laughed.

Gregory didn't answer back. Joey was no fun. Matt was fun. Yet dangerous and a pain in the neck. Besides, he had insulted Dad.

Gregory cranked the window shut. Through the frosted glass, he watched the dark shadow of Matt get smaller. He squeezed his hands into fists so tight his fingernails cut into his palms. It was bad enough that Matt had said things about him, but to say those things against *Dad*. . . .

Was Dad a big chicken? Was that why he hadn't come?

When Gregory looked in the mirror, his face was red. He kept looking at his reflection, opening and closing his hands, until his face returned to its normal pale brown.

To forget Matt, Gregory tried to imagine the Ferris wheel again, but he couldn't.

He slipped on his sneakers without socks and went out to the courtyard. He hadn't attended to the tallies on the back of the Coke machine for days. He scratched out six lines. Only twenty-one days left.

Then he looked up. He almost hadn't noticed the clouds building on the horizon. He'd given up on looking for them, and now they were there like puffy sheep arriving from a great distance.

Maybe the rain right this moment was splashing in big drops on the red ground of Bird Springs, creating red mud, making the junipers and sage smell. Gregory's heart fluttered like a hawk about to take off. The clouds almost made him forget about the fight with Matt.

He went into the room and made himself a peanut butter sandwich with no jelly, then ate it sitting at the small round table. He rinsed his plate in the bathroom sink, then drew a Batman and cut it out. Dad would enjoy these Batmen, if he were only around to see them.

A dark film passed over the front windows as though dusk had suddenly come. Gregory pulled aside the curtains on the front window. Clouds everywhere. In just a short time, the sky had filled with great bundles of them.

The clouds looked heavy and dark on the bottoms, as though they held plenty of rain. Gregory let the curtains fall back. If it rained, Mom wouldn't take him to the carnival tonight. She wouldn't want Jeanine to get wet. But even more than going to the carnival, he longed for rain.

He lay down on the bed, feeling it settle under his weight. He felt Joey lie down beside him. Then he stiffened.

Rain. Matt. Gregory glanced at the glowing red numerals on the clock by the bed: 12:53. Matt would have already entered the tunnel. He might not have noticed the clouds at noon.

The tunnel was a canyon. A canyon like the one at Bird Springs. A canyon where water flowed in a big wave when it rained. In fact, the tunnel was *supposed* to carry water. If a wallawater came, there would be no escape.

Gregory sat up and swung his legs over the edge of the bed. Surely Matt would have checked the sky before going down. He thought back—when had he first been outside? When had he first seen the clouds? Had it been noon, a little before, or a little after? He couldn't remember.

But Matt wouldn't go into the tunnel if it had looked like rain, would he?

Knowing Matt, he probably would.

Gregory kicked his legs back and forth, knocking his heels against the floor. There was no telling what Matt would do.

Forget it. You can't help him, said Joey, still lying down. *We need to be here in case your mom gets back.*

Gregory thought of the tunnel filling with water like the canyon at Bird Springs. The flash flood came suddenly. Uncle Felix said it could even be sunny there in the canyon and *whoosh*—down would come the wallawater from where it was raining someplace else.

It might be raining outside the city from where the clouds came from. At this moment the water could be collecting, ready to pour into the tunnel. Matt wouldn't expect a flash flood.

He thought of Dad and the way he'd been telling everyone that Dad was a warrior. He was Dad's son and a warrior, too.

Joey read his mind. *You'll get in trouble. A bunch of it. Besides, he called your dad a chicken.*

But Gregory didn't listen. He double-knotted his sneakers. *Stay here,* he ordered Joey. He didn't want anyone nagging and interfering.

He had no flashlight.

Shutting the door, he scanned the courtyard for Mr. Hass. He heard a clanging by the Dumpsters. Mr. Hass was probably cleaning up the garbage area.

Gregory crossed the courtyard and opened the

door to the kitchen. No one was cooking for once. On top of the stove he saw the white china dish with the little boxes of matches for lighting the stove. He took a box, shook it to make sure there were enough matches inside, then put the box in his pocket.

17

Outside, the clouds seemed to press down. Gregory could almost feel their weight as he ran. It was as though they were trying to keep him from getting to Matt.

On the way to school, he passed the carnival. The rides had started up. As he ran, Gregory took sideways peeks at the Ferris wheel rolling around and around through the sky.

No one was mowing the lawn at school, thank goodness. Only a few kids were shooting baskets on the opposite side of the playground. Black crows picked through the grass.

Gregory put both hands on the grate and pulled. For a moment the iron bars wouldn't budge. But then the grate lifted free, bits of dried grass sticking to the underside. The opening looked so small. Would he really fit in there? He slipped in, angling his shoulders sideways.

He had to stuff his hands in his pockets to keep them from reaching up to climb out. Then he remembered watching Dad riding Blackie fast, his long hair streaming behind him. Surely Dad would have gone into the tunnel to look for Matt.

Gregory climbed down and struck a match. Then he stopped and listened for water. He heard only the thin shouts of the basketball players above and far away.

The tunnel was totally black. He struck another match, the sulphur stinging his nose. He held the match up and let it burn down until his fingertips were hot.

"Matt!" he shouted. His voice continued to echo, **"Matt**, Matt, Matt," as it traveled down the tunnel.

He waited for Matt's return call to bounce back, but a deep silence wrapped itself around him.

Gregory took a few steps in the darkness, guiding himself with one hand against the wall. When each match burned out, the afterimage glowed against the darkness and made it hard to move forward. If he ran out of matches, and the sun went down, the openings to the street would be blacked out and he wouldn't find them. He would be down here until morning, and by then, surely, the flash flood would have arrived.

Once his cousin Timothy had poured a cup of ice down Gregory's back, underneath his shirt. Now he shivered just like that.

Maybe he should turn back. Maybe Matt wasn't down here after all. He should have checked Matt's house first. Maybe after the skateboarding was over, Matt had gotten interested in another show.

Maybe he was alone.

Gregory waited, letting the idea settle in his mind, listening for either Matt or the wallawater.

Another match burned out. Gregory blinked his eyes, trying to make the afterimage disappear. But the pale yellow glow still hung in the blackness.

The afterimage should have gone away by now, but it hadn't. The glow moved closer. Suddenly afraid, Gregory pressed his body flat against the side of the tunnel. It might be Matt coming or it might be a ghost. On the reservation, everyone believed in ghosts.

Suddenly he wasn't sure he wanted to meet

Matt, either. Was he still angry? As the light drew closer, Gregory saw Matt's pale hand lit dully by the penlight. He hadn't bought a new battery.

Not wanting to scare him, Gregory whispered, "Hey, there."

The light zigzagged upward. Matt's voice sounded zigzaggy, too. "Yikes. You scared me, Greg. That you?"

Gregory lit another match and held it up so that Matt could see him. "It's me, all right." The ice-down-the-back feeling came again. But this time Gregory shivered at his own bravery.

"Hey, cool. You came down after all. My light has a bunch more power left in it. We can explore down another tunnel I found back there." With that, Matt turned off the penlight and the blackness jumped right up.

Matt obviously didn't know about the clouds that had gathered above them. Right now those clouds could be dropping their loads of rain. All those drops might be gathering together into the wallawater.

"No. We got to get out now. That's what I came to tell you. It's raining."

"Rain?" Matt said so loudly that his voice echoed three times, getting smaller as it passed down the tunnel.

Gregory couldn't see Matt's face at all. Was he laughing at the idea? "Yeah. This place is gonna flood."

"Naw. Not here. You're thinking of that mountain place where those kinds of things happen. This tunnel just gets a little water. Like up to our ankles. This is the desert, remember?"

Gregory was glad that Matt couldn't see his face. Was it true what Matt was saying? Had he been foolish to get all excited and rush down here? He said nothing.

Matt didn't say anything, either.

Gregory heard his own heart beating in the blackness of his chest. He thought he heard Matt's heart, too.

"Hey, thanks anyhow," Matt finally said.

"Wasn't nothing," Gregory answered.

"I thought you didn't like me."

"I never said that," Gregory protested. He'd only *thought* about not liking Matt.

"But back at the motel . . ."

"Let's forget about it," Gregory said.

"But you thought about me and got on down here with just them matches."

They were silent again.

"Hey, I know," Matt said suddenly. "I got two dollars. That'd get us each a ride at the carnival. They're done setting it up."

Gregory had forgotten about the carnival. When Matt said the word, his heart stopped its heavy thump and lifted as though he were already soaring high on the big wheel.

"There's still a lot of day left," Matt continued. "That way you don't have to get in trouble."

The walk back to the opening in the school lawn seemed shorter as Gregory followed Matt. Matt swung the light in circles against the walls of the tunnel.

Gregory longed to be above ground. Even more, he longed to sail high into the air on the Ferris wheel.

The daylight coming through the grate looked gray, but no rain was falling. When Matt pushed on the grate, it refused to move, so Gregory reached up both arms to help him and it broke free.

"You get out first," Matt said. "I know you want to." He showed Gregory the shallow footholds in the cement.

When Gregory climbed up, he startled a group of crows that flapped away, the dull light bouncing off their wings. Then he knelt in the green grass and reached down to help Matt.

The clouds looked the same as when he'd first entered the tunnel. At Bird Springs, clouds didn't wait so long to rain. They were like water balloons stretched tight and ready to burst.

18

They left the school's carefully kept grounds and crossed into the vacant lot of prickly tumbleweeds and broken glass. Beyond, the Ferris wheel turned brightly against the dull sky.

At the ticket booth, Matt bought two tickets and handed one to Gregory.

Gregory held the ticket tightly between his thumb and forefinger as they stood in line. The baskets swept down and down. People stepped inside and were swept up and up. When the basket arrived for Gregory and Matt, it was cherry red, just as Gregory had imagined.

They got in, and the man pulled the bar across their laps and locked it firmly with a click.

"Here goes nothing," Matt said.

"Yep, here goes," Gregory answered. He almost moved over to make room for Joey. But Joey wasn't there. As the basket jerked forward, Gregory pictured the room back at the motel. It was empty—no Joey there, either. For a moment, his stomach rose toward his throat.

As the Ferris wheel swung to the top, Gregory could see the cars driving on the freeway, the high buildings downtown, the mountains stretching away and away beyond. Bird Springs was over there in the blue folds of land, underneath the curtain of falling rain. Even if he couldn't see it exactly, he connected with it each time the big wheel reached the top of the arc.

He could see so far that he might be looking at the spot where Dad was living. Although he didn't know the spot, if he looked everywhere, he would be part of the same landscape as Dad.

He imagined the canyon of Bird Springs. Joey was there by the pool, staring at his reflection as though looking for company. Gregory was tempted to call out to him, but then the image faded. Gregory saw nothing but the big buildings to the north, the swirl of traffic on the roads below.

Good bye. Gregory sent Joey one last mind-to-mind message.

"Cool, huh?" said Matt.

"Real cool. Thanks for the ticket."

As they ascended one more time, raindrops began to fall. It was raining at Bird Springs. Gregory lifted his face to the rain, every bit of him thirsty. A healing patter of soft, wet stars had come to him at last.

19

Even though he didn't have to, Gregory got Jeanine from the day care. He felt alive and refreshed from the rain. He whistled as he wheeled the stroller across the courtyard. The clouds formed a heavy gray sheet, and a few drops were still falling.

He laid Jeanine on Mom's bed and brought her a rattle and her stuffed monkey. He shook the monkey's tail, and Jeanine giggled.

Now that the rains had come, Timothy and Susanna, Uncle Felix, and the rest of the relatives might go back to Bird Springs. They could all have a party to celebrate. Standing Rock might have water. The streams would be flowing, red mud eddying into them.

Jeanine chewed on the rattle, gurgled, and slept.

Gregory tried to do his English homework on avoiding double negatives but kept going back and forth to the window, pulling aside the curtains, waiting for Mom.

At last he heard her footsteps on the path. He swung the door open wide. "Isn't it great?"

"What's great, hon?" Mom slid her purse off her shoulder.

"The *rain*."

She looked at the sky. "It *was* nice. While it lasted."

Gregory moved back so that Mom could come in. "So when can we go to Bird Springs?"

Mom dropped her purse onto the chair. "What do you mean?"

"It rained, didn't it?"

"A few drops, Gregory. Not much."

"But it'll rain more, won't it?"

"It'll have to rain for a very long time before we go back."

"Maybe it will."

She sighed. "Even if it rains buckets, you know we can't live there without your dad."

In the excitement of the Ferris wheel ride, he'd forgotten that part. Without Dad, they couldn't get water to the cabin, even if every stream flooded its banks. He kicked at the fringe hanging down from the blue bedspread.

"I'm sorry, honey." Mom laid a cool hand on the back of his neck. "I know you miss your home."

Mom even worked on Sunday. "Nights and weekends," she said. "That's my job."

After breakfast, Gregory left the motel, walking down the path and out the front gate. The clouds had drifted off without dropping any more rain. A gray film coated the sky.

As he passed the school, Gregory wondered if Ms. Daniels was inside, getting ready for Monday. He imagined her quietly folding bright tissue paper, lining up the colored chalks, pressing the clay into its bucket. She might need his help. But the lights were off inside the classroom, the drapes pulled.

He walked on to the carnival, where he'd agreed to meet Matt. He found him watching a girl and a man trying to toss rings over the necks of bottles.

"I wish I could win that." Matt pointed to the wall behind the bottles, at a fuzzy pink snake with enormous eyelashes.

"For what?"

"Just to have."

Gregory glanced up at the Ferris wheel.

"I'm outta money," Matt said, "in case you got any ideas of riding that again."

As they strolled around the carnival, Gregory noticed the empty space beside him where Joey had been. He felt a little twinge of missing him, but then looked at Matt, blond and solid, beside him.

They watched the green boats full of little kids who thought they were actually steering, and passed close to people eating cotton candy, hungrily sniffing the sugary sweetness. They watched the arc of the slim metal darts, heard the thuds of their landing.

"It's a drag not having money to spend," Matt finally said.

"Let's hang out at school." Gregory wanted to be close to Ms. Daniels's room, the place she made hers.

When they got to school, they scrambled to the top of the climber, standing to balance on the uppermost bars—something the playground monitors never would have allowed.

"King of the World," declared Matt, raising both fists.

Gregory wobbled a little as he tried to see up north, to the sky above Bird Springs. Was it cloudy up there, or did the pale haze go on and on? He couldn't tell.

They slipped down, hand over hand, through the web of metal bars. Matt jumped to the ground and Gregory followed.

"Let's go lie on the grass," Gregory said. "At Bird Springs we don't have any."

Matt shook his head. "You Indian guys are so weird."

Gregory guided Matt to the spot underneath Ms. Daniels's window. Two black crows fluttered off.

"Do you think it'll rain again?" Gregory asked, looking up at the gray sky.

"Beats me."

They lay in the grass underneath the window. Gregory loved the soft, prickly feel through his shirt. He loved the coolness.

"What do you think of her?" Gregory asked, ͏ting a blade of grass between his thumb and ͏͏er.

͏͏r."

͏e art *therapy* teacher? She's okay."

"Don't you think she's pretty?"

"She's old. Gross."

The words felt like small flung pebbles. Gregory winced. "She doesn't look old."

"But she is. At least twenty. You like her?"

Gregory leaned up onto one elbow. "Sort of."

Matt chewed on a blade of grass. "If you like her, you better clean up."

"Like what?"

"Like get a haircut."

"Mr. Hass gave me a coupon."

"So what're ya waiting for?"

"I don't know if I want to cut it off or leave it long, like my dad's."

"Indian style, you mean?"

"Yeah." Gregory turned his head to see the black crows moving closer.

"If you like her," Matt said, "you gotta give her something really special."

"Like what?"

"Girls like jewelry."

Jewelry. And then it came to him. He did have something special. Something from the heart of Bird Springs.

That night, while Mom was working, he got the necklace out of its hiding place in the toilet tank and dried it with a towel.

Jeanine watched, bright-eyed, from the bed.

"Don't tell Mom," he said to her, wrapping the treasure in a washcloth, tucking it deep into his backpack. "Don't be a tattletale."

After school, when Ms. Daniels opened the wash-cloth, and the necklace lay exposed on her lap, Gregory noticed that the tarnished silver needed polishing. But the stones were still pure chunks of sky. She stared, just as he'd hoped she would. "It's beautiful," she said at last.

"You can borrow it for a while."

She hande
water and th
what you sa

Behind
kind of exp
not good a
"You c
Paint it th
He st
"Wh

He
cabin.
too, e
wanti
into

of
ad
p

Ms. Daniels was right. Dad would never come.

Once, when Gregory had been swimming, the river below Standing Rock had carried him and let him go. The current had ended and he'd been left in stillness. He was stuck in that stillness again.

"And you love him, too," she added. "I can see that."

He nodded and coughed again.

"Gregory. There's something I want to show you. Open your hand."

He unclenched his fingers. The inside of his hand was paler than the outside, like something hidden from the light.

"Gregory, your dad is in you. His genes are in you. Whenever you want to see him, look into your own palm."

Gregory stared into his hand, at the lines that ran like dry riverbeds.

Ms. Daniels looked into his hand, too, as though she were also searching for Dad.

The clock ticked.

"That's your father's hand, Gregory," she finally said. "Even if he's left you, he remains in your body."

He saw the long fingers of Dad's hand. And

somehow the skin, and the bones inside, were a continuation of Dad. He closed his fingers carefully over his palm.

He looked up at her, eyes red, nose sniffly. Not the warrior he'd imagined. "Thank you, miss."

She laughed. "You're very welcome, Gregory. Want to try another experiment?"

"I guess," he said, staring down at the shoes that pinched his toes. Then he asked, "Was it because of Dad that you chose me to be in this class?"

Ms. Daniels stared for a moment, as though she didn't understand. Then she shook her head. "Oh, no. I had no way of knowing about that. You were put in here because of your address. Because of the shelter. Kids who live at the shelter need a little fun in their lives. That's all."

A knot within him loosened. "So I'm not screwed up?"

She laughed quickly. "Who told you that?" "Matt."

"That Matt. No, Gregory, you're not screwe... You're here because of your living situatio...

He sat a moment with the inform... seep in the way water seeped b...

he took a big breath and said, "How about that experiment?"

While Ms. Daniels was wetting another piece of paper, Gregory rolled up his sleeve so the snot wouldn't show.

She brought the paper. "I want you to paint not just the house you used to live in, but the colors of the place around it, the feelings it gave you when you lived there."

He sat without moving.

"Go on. Don't worry."

He reached for the blue. The blue of the sky. He dropped globs onto the wet paper. He liked the way the water made the paint look like real sky—not solid blue, but an uneven blueness.

"What else?" she asked.

"Red." He looked around the room until he saw a terra-cotta pot holding a green vine. "Like that," he pointed.

"I'll help you mix." She dipped the brush quickly ⌐n the red, the jar of water, the yellow, the water, ⌐ntil she'd created the color of the pot.

⌐ strokes, he swept the color below

"Another color?"

"Dark green. Like pine trees."

"You can mix that, Gregory. Here, try a little of this and this and this." She pointed to the paints.

At first his green was too yellow, then too blue, but finally he arrived at a puddle of piñon pine green. He used just a little, dotting it into the drier patches of red.

Finally he painted yellow for the roadside flowers that had blocked their way.

"I want to make rain," he said. He went to the sink, emptied the now-muddy jar of water, and brought back clear water. He dipped his brush in the jar and sprinkled droplets over the painting.

"This looks like a happy place," Ms. Daniels said, staring at the sea of colors. "What is it called?"

"Bird Springs."

"What a beautiful name."

"It's a beautiful place. Maybe someday," he said, "you'll visit it."

"I'd love to, Gregory." She looked at the clock. "You've been very brave this afternoon. I hope it wasn't too hard."

He nodded, biting the inside of his cheek.

She reached up to unclasp the necklace.

Again, he wished she'd have trouble, but she swung the two ends down and handed the necklace back.

Instead of wrapping the necklace in the wash-cloth, he held it in both hands, absorbing the warmth from her neck.

Gregory stepped out of the classroom into the sun of late afternoon. He paused, surveying the blades of grass catching the light, the crows shuttling back and forth to the trees. Below lay the maze of tunnels, secretly dark.

He carried his backpack over one shoulder, the necklace of heavy stones in his hand.

Joey was gone. Dad would never come back.

And yet, strangely, he felt light. Light and full of possibility, like the moment when the Ferris wheel basket paused at the top of the arc.

He was ready for a haircut.

Gregory walked to the main street, the slits in the curb that led down t